Tales of
Nonsense
& Tomfoolery

Also by Pleasant DeSpain

THE BOOKS OF NINE LIVES

VOLUME TWO

Tales of
Nonsense
& Tomfoolery

Pleasant DeSpain

Illustrations by Don Bell

August House Publishers, Inc.
LITTLE ROCK

S

J
398.2
DES

Published 2001 by August House Publishers, Inc.
P.O. Box 3223, Little Rock, Arkansas, 72203,
501-372-5450.

Printed in the United States of America

10 9 8 7 6 5 4 3 2 1 PB

LIBRARY OF CONGRESS CATALOGING-IN-PUBLICATION DATA

DeSpain, Pleasant.
  Tales of nonsense & tomfoolery / Pleasant DeSpain ; illustrations by Don Bell.
    p. cm. — (The books of nine lives ; v. 2)
  Summary: A collection of short folktales featuring silly characters, nonsen-
  sical situations, or general tomfoolery.
  ISBN 0-87483-645-X (alk. paper)
  1. Tales. [1. Folklore.] I. Title: Tales of nonsense and tomfoolery. II. Bell,
  Don, 1935- ill. III. Title.
  PZ8.1.D453 Tal 2001
  398.2   2001022118

Executive editor: Liz Parkhurst
Project editor & designer: Joy Freeman
Copyeditor: Sue Agnelli
Cover and book illustration: Don Bell

The paper used in this publication meets the minimum requirements
of the American National Standard for Information Sciences—
Permanence of Paper for Printed Library Materials, ANSI Z39.48–1984.

AUGUST HOUSE   PUBLISHERS   LITTLE ROCK

For Eleanor J. Feazell and Edward E. Feazell,
my mother and stepfather.
You are loved and appreciated, always.

Acknowledgments

I'm fortunate to have genuine friends and colleagues without whose help, the first three editions of these tales would not have been possible. Profound thanks to: Leslie Gillian Abel, Ruthmarie Arguello-Sheehan, Merle and Anne Dowd, Edward Edelstein, Rufus Griscom, Robert Guy, Daniel Higgins, Roger Lanphear, Kirk Lyttle, Liz and Ted Parkhurst, Lynn Rubright, Mason Sizemore, Perrin Stifel, Paul Thompson, and T.R. Welch.

I owe allegiance and appreciation to the following for the newest incarnation:

Liz and Ted Parkhurst, Publishers
Don Bell, Illustrator
Joy Freeman, Project Editor

The Books of Nine Lives Series

A good story lives each time it's read and told again. The stories in this series have had many lives over the centuries. My own retellings of the tales in this volume have had several lives in the past twenty plus years, and I'm pleased to witness their new look and feel. Originally published in "Pleasant Journeys," my weekly column in *The Seattle Times,* during 1977–78, they were collected into a two-volume set entitled *Pleasant Journeys, Tales to Tell from Around the World,* in 1979. The books were renamed *Twenty-Two Splendid Tales to Tell From Around the World,* a few years later, and have remained in print for twenty-one years and three editions.

Now, in 2001, the time has come for a new presentation of these timeless, ageless, universal, useful, and so very human tales.

The first three multicultural and thematically based volumes are just the beginning. Volumes four, five, and six will soon follow, and even more volumes are planned for the future, offering additional timeless tales.

I'm profoundly grateful to all the teachers, parents, storytellers and children who have found these tales worthy of sharing. One story always leads to the next. May these lead you to laughter, wisdom, and love. As evolving, planetary, and human beings, we are more alike than we are different, each with a story to tell.

—Pleasant DeSpain
Albany, New York

Contents

Introduction

I love the word *tomfoolery*. It means doing something silly or foolish or being a noodlehead. Tales of foolishness are not only fun, but found throughout the world. Every culture known to humankind has its fools. We can learn from telling their stories how not to be one. Yet we must all be a little silly, or foolish, or even a noodlehead, once in a while. What would our lives be without smiles and belly laughs? These tales help us remember the importance of the fools' role in society.

I've traveled to every state in the United States and all around the world searching for, telling, and listening to stories. I've found scary stories and wise stories. I've found tales of adventure and love. I've found myths about heroes and heroines of old. But the stories I've enjoyed sharing the most are the ones that make me laugh.

The tales in this collection make me laugh. From Russia to Ethiopia, from China to Norway, from the United States to India, these are universal tales that are fun to read, and learn to tell, again and again. As I've always said, the world needs more tellers of tales, especially the funny ones.

The Turnip

Russia

One day Grandfather planted a turnip in his garden. It grew and grew and grew, and when it came time to pull it out of the ground, it was huge!

Grandfather pulled and pulled, but he couldn't pull it out of the ground.

"Grandmother, come and help me pull up this turnip!" called Grandfather.

Grandmother pulled on Grandfather and Grandfather pulled on the turnip. They pulled and pulled, but they couldn't pull it out of the ground.

Grandmother called to Mother, "Come and help us pull up this turnip."

Mother pulled on Grandmother, Grandmother pulled on Grandfather, and Grandfather pulled on the turnip. They pulled and they pulled, but the turnip wouldn't budge.

"Daughter," called Mother, "come and help us pull up this turnip!"

Daughter pulled on Mother, Mother pulled on Grandmother, Grandmother pulled on Grandfather, and Grandfather pulled on the turnip. They pulled and they pulled, but it wouldn't move.

Daughter called to the dog, "Come and help us pull up this turnip!"

The dog pulled on Daughter, Daughter pulled on Mother, Mother pulled on Grandmother, Grandmother pulled on Grandfather, and Grandfather pulled on the turnip. They pulled and they pulled, but the turnip still wouldn't budge.

The dog barked to the cat, "Come and help us pull up this turnip!"

The cat pulled on the dog, the dog pulled on Daughter, Daughter pulled on Mother, Mother pulled on Grandmother, Grandmother pulled on Grandfather, and Grandfather pulled on the turnip. They pulled and they pulled, but they couldn't pull it out of the ground.

The cat meowed to the mouse, "Come and help us pull up this turnip!"

The mouse pulled on the cat, the cat pulled on the dog, the dog pulled on Daughter, Daughter pulled on Mother, Mother pulled on Grandmother, Grandmother pulled on Grandfather, and Grandfather pulled on the turnip. They pulled and they pulled, but they couldn't pull the turnip out of the ground.

The mouse squeaked to the beetle, "Come and help us pull up this turnip!" The beetle pulled on the mouse, the mouse pulled on the cat, the cat pulled on the dog, the dog pulled on Daughter, Daughter pulled on Mother, Mother pulled on Grandmother, Grandmother pulled on Grandfather, and Grandfather pulled on the turnip. They pulled and they pulled, and they pulled the huge turnip right up out of the ground!

The turnip was so large that it fell on Grandfather and knocked him over! Grandfather fell on Grandmother! Grandmother fell on Mother! Mother fell on Daughter! Daughter fell on the dog! The dog fell on the cat! The cat fell on the mouse! The mouse fell on the beetle! And they all ate the turnip for supper.

The Silly Farmer

Ethiopia

A silly farmer named Zaheed lived in Ethiopia. One day his wife told him that she was going to have a baby. Zaheed asked her what kind of baby it would be, but she didn't know.

"Then," said Zaheed, "I will visit the wise old woman who lives at the base of the mountains. She has magic, both black and white, and she will be able to tell me."

He took a gold piece that he had hidden deep in his straw mattress and walked all morning until he reached the old witch's hut.

"I've come to ask you a difficult question," said Zaheed. "If you can give me a satisfactory answer, I'll pay you with this piece of gold."

The old woman stared at him with dark eyes and nodded her head in agreement.

"My wife is going to have a child, but she doesn't know what kind it will be. Can you tell me?"

The old woman opened a small wooden chest and removed three ancient bones. She tossed them on the ground and studied the pattern they made. She shook her head and said, "Ehh."

Zaheed also shook his head and said, "Ehh."

She tossed them again, studied the pattern, and said, "Ahh!"

"Ahh!" repeated Zaheed.

Once more she tossed the bones and studied the pattern. "Of course!" she exclaimed.

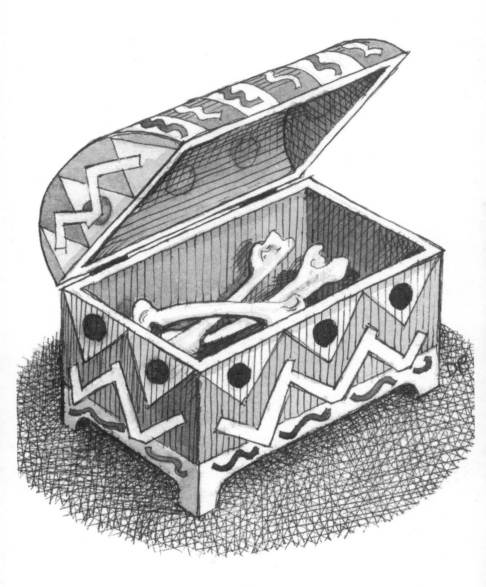

"Of course!" shouted Zaheed.

"Your wife's child will be either a boy or a girl."

"How wonderful!" said Zaheed. He gave the witch the gold and ran home to tell his wife the good news.

Several months later, his wife had a fat baby girl. "You see," Zaheed told all of his neighbors, "the old woman was right!"

Soon it was time to baptize the girl, but Zaheed and his wife couldn't think of a proper name for her.

"I'll go ask the old woman," said Zaheed. "She is wise and will tell me our daughter's name."

He took another piece of gold from the mattress and walked back to the witch's hut. After Zaheed explained the problem, the old woman took the bones from the chest and tossed them onto the floor. "Ahh!" said she.

"Ahh!" said Zaheed.

Again she tossed the bones. "Of course!"

"Of course!" repeated Zaheed.

"Give me the gold," said the witch, "and I will whisper the child's name into your hands."

Zaheed did as she said and extended his hands. She quickly whispered into them and said, "Now close your hands tight so that you won't lose the name on the way home."

The farmer ran toward home with his hands clasped together. When he came to his neighbor's farm, he saw several of the men pitching hay into tall stacks. "I have it! I have it!" he cried. "The name of my daughter is here in my hands!" Just then he slipped on some loose hay and fell to the ground. His hands came apart, and he yelled, "Now I've lost it! Quickly, help me find it again!"

Several of the men ran up and helped Zaheed search through the haystack with their pitchforks.

Soon after, a woman from the village

walked by and asked what they were looking for. Zaheed explained how the witch had given him the name and how he had lost it.

"It is nonsense!" she declared. "Simply nonsense!"

"Oh, thank you!" said Zaheed. "I thought I had lost it forever."

When he got home, the silly farmer explained everything to his wife. "The witch whispered the name into my hands, but I lost it on the way home. The neighbor woman found it and told it to me. Our daughter's name is Nonsense! Simply Nonsense!"

And they call her Simply Nonsense to this very day.

Close the Door!

United States

There once lived a husband and wife who were stubborn. While having supper one night, a strong gust of wind blew the cottage door wide open.

"Husband," said the woman, "get up and close the door before the wind blows our meat and potatoes onto the floor."

"You close it, wife. I worked in the fields all day and I'm tired."

"I worked all day as well," said the wife. "You close it."

"My work is harder than yours and I want

you to close the door!" yelled the man.

"No!" said the wife. "My work doesn't end at sundown, like yours. You close it!"

"Wife, you are as stubborn as our mule!"

"Husband, you are worse!"

They both knew that neither one would win the argument, so they agreed to be silent. They also agreed that the first to break the silence by speaking would have to close the door against the cold night wind. They remained silent for hours, and when it was time to go to bed, they crawled under the covers without a word.

A thief who was both cold and hungry happened by. He thought it strange to find the door wide open, a cold fireplace, and the man and woman in bed with their eyes open wide and their mouths shut tight.

"Good evening," said the thief, "could you spare a crust of bread for a hungry man?"

Absolute silence was the reply.

"What's that you say?" asked the thief, "Help myself to all the food I want?"

He wasted no time in placing all the food in the house on the tablecloth and wrapping it up into a large bundle.

"And now, would you happen to have an old coat to spare, to help keep the chill from my bones?" asked the thief.

The silence continued.

"Why, thank you, I will take whatever I can use," said the thief, and he emptied the closets and made a second bundle.

"Before I leave, my friends, could I trouble you for a coin or two? What's that? Take all I can find? You're too kind!" said the thief, smiling.

The thief searched throughout the cottage and found all the money that had been hidden away. Thinking that he must have a little more fun with this foolish couple, he went to the fireplace and filled his hands with soot.

"Here's a little gift for you, my quiet friends," said the thief, and he smeared the soot all over the woman's face.

Neither husband nor wife said a word.

The thief picked up the bundles of food and clothing and, his pockets heavy with coins, walked out of the cottage.

The man and woman lay in bed the rest of the night without speaking. The door to their cottage still stood wide open.

The next morning, the birds sang a cheery song as the sun rose in the eastern sky. The couple sat up in bed, and the man looked at his wife.

"Wife, your face is all black!" he exclaimed.

"Husband, you spoke first. Get up and close the door!" she said triumphantly. And they lived stubbornly ever after.

The Squire's Bride

Norway

Long ago in Norway, there lived a wealthy squire named Jensen. He owned the largest farm in the valley and had money in the bank. He should have been happy, but because he was old and lived alone, he wasn't.

Thus he decided to marry the young daughter of his poor neighbor, Farmer Patterson. Her name was Ingrid, and she was the prettiest as well as the most stubborn girl in the valley.

The next day the old squire walked to his

neighbor's barnyard and found the girl feeding the chickens.

"I've been thinking of getting married, my dear Ingrid—that is, if you'll agree."

"Me, marry you?" laughed Ingrid. "Don't be foolish; you're much too old for me."

Now Squire Jensen was used to having his own way. He went to her father and said, "Neighbor Patterson, you owe me three hundred kroner and two cows. If you will convince your daughter to marry me, I'll pay for the wedding and forget the debt. If not, I'll buy your farm out from under you."

"Don't you worry, Squire," said the farmer. "Ingrid will see reason soon enough." He was very worried about his farm and thought that he could talk his daughter into the marriage.

"No! No! No!" cried Ingrid when he spoke with her. "I will not marry that old man! Even if he owned every farm in the valley, I would not be his bride!"

The next day Farmer Patterson explained to Squire Jensen, "My daughter is thinking it over. She will soon come to the right decision."

"She must decide by tomorrow, or your debt becomes due," the squire declared.

Since Farmer Patterson didn't have the money or the cows, he had to tell the squire that Ingrid had at last agreed and only hope that she would change her mind before the wedding day.

On the next day, he said to the squire, "Ingrid will marry you, but you must keep the wedding dress and crown at your house. Invite all the neighbors, and when the parson is ready, send for my daughter. Have the women help her dress, and you'll be married before she can change her mind." The squire was pleased.

During the next week, the squire's servants cleaned and baked night and day in order to have everything ready. When the guests and the parson were assembled, the squire sent one of his farm boys to find Farmer Patterson.

"My master sent me to fetch what you two talked about," said the boy to Ingrid's father.

Farmer Patterson crossed his fingers for luck and said, "She is down in the hayfield, lad."

The boy ran to the hayfield and found Ingrid feeding a little bay mare. "I've come for what the squire and your father talked about."

Ingrid guessed what was happening and said, "I hate to give her up, but if the squire wants my mare, then he shall have her."

The boy rode the horse to the back door of the squire's mansion, leaped to the ground, and ran inside.

"Is she here?" the squire asked anxiously.

The boy nodded.

"Then take her up the back stairs to the large bedroom."

"But why?" asked the confused boy.

"Don't ask any questions! Have the farmhands help you if she is troublesome."

It took several of the men to push and pull the frightened mare up the stairs and into the bedroom. On the bed lay a beautiful wedding dress and crown.

The boy ran back to the squire and said, "We have her upstairs, Master."

"Send the women in to help her dress. Ask no questions and tell the women to be quick about it."

The women giggled when they heard the order, but supposed that it was all a joke to make the guests laugh. They had to split the dress down the back and drape it over the reluctant horse and tie the crown on her head. When she was ready, the boy ran to tell the squire.

"Bring her down and the wedding will begin," said the squire proudly.

There was a terrible clatter of hoofs on the stairs and the squire's mouth fell open when the bride, looking very much like a horse, appeared. The guests began to laugh, and they laughed until they cried.

Old Squire Jensen became the laughing-stock of the valley, and never again did he ask a young girl to be his bride.

The Extraordinary Cat

China

Once there was a Chinese ruler who had a cat that he treasured above all other animals. He loved the cat so much and thought that it was so extraordinary that he named it Sky.

One day soon after, an advisor to the court spoke to the ruler and explained, "There is something much more powerful than the sky, and that is the cloud. The cloud can darken and even hide the sky from view."

"Quite right," agreed the ruler. "From this day forth, my beautiful cat shall be called Cloud."

Two weeks later the ruler's wife said, "Dear husband, I don't think that Cloud is a proper name for your cat. There is something stronger than the cloud, and that is the wind that blows the cloud about."

"Indeed! From now on, my superior cat will be called Wind. Here Wind! Here Wind! Nice little Wind."

During the next month, the ruler's brother came for a visit and agreed that the cat was the most extraordinary animal he had ever seen. "But," he said, "Wind is not a suitable name for this superb creature. The wind is servant to that which it cannot penetrate... such as a wall. The wall is stronger than the wind."

I hadn't thought of that," replied the ruler, "and you are to be congratulated, brother, for being so observant. From now on, my dearest cat, the most wonderful cat on earth, will be called Wall.

The very next day the royal gardener heard the ruler call his cat, "Wall," and said, "But sire, you are forgetting that a mouse is able to chew a hole in a wall. The mouse is the strongest."

"How clever of you," said the ruler. "From this day forth, my lovely cat will be called Mouse. Come here Mouse!"

But just then the ruler's boy and girl skipped into the garden to play, and when they heard their father call the cat, "Mouse," they started to laugh and laugh!

"What causes you to laugh, children?" asked the ruler.

"Father," replied the little girl, "everyone knows that there is something stronger than the mouse, and that's the cat who catches it!"

The ruler smiled as he realized that his children were the wisest of all his advisors. Then he began to laugh. "Of course! How

foolish I've been. From now on my extraordinary animal will be called by the name
he most deserves, and that is Cat!"

The Man Who Was on Fire Behind

Switzerland

Once there was a man named William who liked to play tricks on his neighbors. On more than one occasion, his neighbors returned home to find their chickens locked in the clothes closet or their goats up on the roof. One neighbor even found a goldfish in his drinking water!

In the next village, there lived a clever young woman named Greta. One afternoon, while she was preparing dinner, William knocked on her door and asked for a drink

of water. Greta recognized him at once and said, "Of course—come in and rest yourself by the warm fire, while I go to the well and fetch a fresh bucket." She didn't let on that she knew who he was, but all the people of her village had heard of William's funny pranks.

While she was gone, William examined everything in the kitchen. He felt the bread dough rising in the pans on the windowsill; he peeked into the tall cookie jar and helped himself to a fresh oatmeal cookie; and he lifted the lid from the large black kettle hanging over the burning logs in the fire-place. A delicious odor rose from inside the pot and tickled his nose. Thick chunks of beef were browning nicely for Greta's supper.

William quickly stabbed the largest chunk of meat and put it into his knapsack, which lay on the floor.

When Greta returned with the water, she

noticed that a faint wisp of steam carrying the odor of cooked beef escaped from the knapsack. She thought for a moment and said, "Now, kind friend, I must ask a favor of you. I need more wood for my fire. Please carry an armload in from the woodshed."

William agreed. While he was gone, Greta took the beef from his knapsack and plopped it back into the kettle. Then she took a smoldering piece of wood from the fire and stuffed it into the leather sack.

William returned with the wood and was anxious to be on his way. He quickly threw the knapsack over his shoulder and started walking toward his village.

"The beef is still good and hot," he said to himself. "I can feel it on my back, right through the leather. How tasty it will be!" The piece of burning wood grew hotter and hotter, and William began to run. As he got close to home, his back seemed to be on fire!

Two neighbors yelled at him as he passed by, "Hey, William, what is that smoking on your back?"

"My dinner!" he replied.

"Your dinner has set your backside on fire!" the neighbors laughed. "And it has burned the back of your coat and the seat of your pants!"

William ran for the nearest duck pond and jumped in. The water hissed and steamed as a white mist rose from his backside.

For many weeks to follow, the villagers teased him by saying, "Hey, William, are you on fire behind?"

He had learned his lesson, and never again did William play tricks on his neighbors.

Two Wives

India

Once there was a man who had the great misfortune of marrying two wives. He soon learned that if he wanted to keep peace in the family, he could not favor one more than the other.

One quiet afternoon, all three were sitting in the garden, resting from the heat of the midday sun. One of the wives was combing her husband's black hair and saw a single white one. She quickly yanked it out.

"Ow!" cried the man. "What are you doing?"

"I found a white hair and pulled it out,"

49

said the first wife.

The second wife spoke up and said, "Foolish woman! A white hair is the sign of approaching wisdom. How dare you pull it out!"

"If it is a sign of wisdom," explained the first wife, "I shall keep it with me always."

"It is not right," complained the second wife, "that you should have a hair while I have none!"

The husband tried to stop the argument by saying, "Dear wives of mine, please don't argue. It is only fair that since my first wife found the white hair, it shall be hers to keep. And it is only fair that since my second wife has none, she shall pull out one of my black hairs. Then each of you will have one."

As soon as the second wife yanked out a black hair, the first wife said, "But husband, she has a black one and mine is white. I, too, want a black one."

"Very well," said the man. "Pull a black hair from my head and be satisfied."

As soon as she plucked the hair, the second wife said angrily, "But she has both a black and a white hair. I have only one black. It isn't fair!"

"You are quite right, my dearest," said the husband. "Simply pull one more hair from my head and you will each have two."

That made the first wife even more jealous. "Now she has two black hairs and I have only one. It is not right, husband, for you to love her more than you love me."

"I'm sorry, sweet wife," said the man whose head was beginning to hurt. "You must take another black one."

Then the second wife screamed, "She has three hairs and I have two! I want three as well!"

"Yes, yes, you may take one more, my dearest," said the poor man.

But of course that dissatisfied the first wife and she had to have another hair. And to keep peace the husband had to give the second wife yet another.

The argument lasted all afternoon with both wives yanking the hairs from his head until at last he was completely bald!

Even though the poor man's head ached, he smiled happily, for now the argument was over and both of his wives were silent.

The Bear Who Said North

Finland

Once upon a time, long, long ago, a lumbering, clumsy old bear caught a fat grouse. The bear was so proud of his achievement that he held the frightened bird with his teeth, being very careful not to harm it. This way he could walk through the forest showing all the other animals that he wasn't such a foolish bear after all.

"The others say I'm just a silly old bear, but when they see that I've caught this fine fat bird they will change their tune," he thought.

He began his proud walk along a heavily traveled forest trail and found the clever fox napping in the shade of a pine tree.

"Umph! Umph!" grunted the bear, trying to attract the fox's attention.

"Oh, go growl to the squirrels, you inconsiderate old fool. Can't you see that I'm having a sweet dream?" complained the fox.

"Umgh! Umgh!" the bear grunted even louder, for he especially wanted the fox to see his triumph.

The fox barely opened one eye and saw that his old enemy was showing off. This made him even more angry, and he decided to play a trick on the bear for disturbing his nap. He yawned and opened his eyes, but he didn't look up at the bear. Instead, he pointed his nose to the ground and sniffed two or three times, being careful not to see the grouse caught in the bear's teeth.

"Tell me, friend," said the fox, "which way

is the wind blowing just now?"

The bear couldn't answer without opening his mouth, and if he opened his mouth, the bird would fly away.

"Umph!' he grunted again, hoping that the fox would look up and see his captive.

"I believe it must be blowing from the west. Yes, it is blowing from the west, isn't that right, friend bear?"

"Umph! Umph! Umph!" said the bear, growing quite angry with the fox.

"What's that? You say it is from the west? But are you sure? Perhaps it is blowing from the south instead."

"Umph!" repeated the bear, growing more and more impatient with the fox.

"The south it is then, after all," said the fox. "But tell me, how did you figure it out?"

By now the bear was so exasperated with the fox that he momentarily forgot himself and opened his mouth to roar, "North! The wind is blowing from the north!"

The grouse flapped her wings the instant his mouth opened and flew to the safety of a high branch.

"Look at what you've made me do!" exclaimed the bear. "My fat bird has escaped and it's all your fault!"

"My fault?" asked the fox innocently. "Why is it my fault?"

"Because you kept asking me about the direction of the wind until I had to open my mouth to answer!"

"But friend bear, why did you open your mouth to answer?" asked the fox.

"Because you can't say 'North!' without opening your mouth," said the unhappy bear.

The fox smiled and said, "If I had caught the grouse and you asked me the direction of the wind, I would not have answered 'North!'"

"Then what would you have said?" asked the bear.

The fox clenched his teeth together and said, "East!"

The Proud Fox

United States

Once upon a time, a proud fox was
taking a leisurely walk through the
forest when a pack of wild dogs caught his
scent and started to chase after him, yelping
and howling as they ran. The fox knew that
he was the fastest runner in the land and
enjoyed the prospect of outwitting the dogs
as he had before. He leaped into the air and
bounded through the forest towards his den.

But the dogs were larger than the fox and
nearly as swift, and they were able to cut off
his path to the den and force him to run back

out of the woods towards the open plains. The fox ran even harder and faster, but the dogs were strong and began to gain on him. Now he was running for his life and he looked desperately for a place to hide!

The plains were vast and he was surrounded by open space. The pack of dogs was howling wildly and they were so close that they were nipping at his bushy tail! Just then, the fox saw a small cave in a large pile of boulders and headed straight for it. The dogs stayed with him and very nearly caught him, but the fox bounded through the rocks and dove into the dark cave!

Fortunately the cave was small—too small for the dogs to enter. They barked and whined and pawed at the ground, but soon they quieted down and all was still.

Now that the fox was safe, he began to feel quite proud of himself once again. He wanted to boast of his skillful run, but there

was no one in the cave to listen to him. So
he began a conversation with the separate
parts of his body.

"Feet, what did you do to help me win the
race?" asked the fox.

"We leaped into the air and carried you
ahead of those mean dogs," said his feet. "We
ran faster than ever before and brought you
to this cave."

"Excellent! You are good feet and I'm proud
of all of you. Now, ears, what was your role?"

"We heard the dogs coming and told the
feet to start running," replied the ears.

"Very well done!" said the fox. "And now,
my eyes. What did you do to help?"

"We found the path to follow. We looked to
the right and to the left, and we saw this
cave in the rocks."

"Wonderful! Just wonderful! What a
splendid fox I am to have such excellent
feet, ears, and eyes!"

"Ah-hem," said the tail, "aren't you forgetting me?"

"Oh yes," said the fox, "how could I forget you, my friendly tail? After all, wasn't it you who almost got me caught by letting the dogs nip at the end of you? Or did you help in some other way that I'm not aware of?"

That made the tail so angry that it said, "I also helped by waving in the air, urging the dogs forward so that they could catch you!"

"Enough!" cried the fox. "How dare you mock me! You are not brave like the others. You are a coward and do not belong in the safety of this cave with the rest of us! Outside with you, traitor! Out! Out you go!"

And the fox backed his tail out of the cave's entrance. The dogs, who were hidden in the rocks, immediately pounced upon it, and that was the end of the proud fox.

Three Wishes

Sweden

Once a poor woodcutter went to the forest to chop down trees. Just as he raised his stout ax to a large old pine, a wood nymph called down from a high branch.

"Please don't harm this tree. It is my home!" she pleaded.

"Very well," said the man, and he lowered the ax.

"Thank you, Woodcutter," said the nymph, "and because you are such a decent fellow, your next three wishes will be answered."

The woodcutter worked hard the rest of

the day and was hungry by the time he arrived at his humble cottage. Since he really didn't believe in magic, he had forgotten about the wood nymph's wishes.

He sat at the table and his wife placed a bowl of weak broth and a hard crust of brown bread in front of him.

"What? Is this all there is for my supper? How I wish I had a nice fat sausage to eat with it," he said.

As soon as the words were spoken, a large sausage appeared on his plate.

"Bless my soul!" cried his wife. "Where did that come from?"

Then the woodcutter remembered what the wood nymph had said about the three wishes, and he told his wife what had happened in the forest that morning.

"And now you've wasted a perfectly good wish on a sausage! You are the most foolish man I've ever heard of. You know how much we need a nicer cottage and a team of horses and money to pay taxes with! And what do you wish for? A sausage, a stupid sausage, that's what you wish for!"

"How you go on about it," said the wood-cutter. "I wish the sausage would stick to your nose!"

No sooner had he said it than the sausage flew up from the plate and landed on the end of the wife's nose. She tried to pull it off, but it wouldn't budge. Her husband tried too, but no matter how hard he pulled, it wouldn't come off.

"Hurry and use your last wish to get it off," demanded the wife. "I can't stand to have such a long nose."

"But what about our new cottage and all the money we need? Wouldn't it be better to have those things?"

His wife shook her head and looked so unhappy with the long sausage hanging

down from her nose that the woodcutter
said, "Then don't you ever say I wasted the
last wish. I wish the sausage gone!"

It vanished in an instant, and with it so
did all the riches the two of them might have
had.

Notes

The stories in this collection are my retellings of tales from throughout the world. They have come to me from written and oral sources, and result from thirty years of my telling them aloud.

All of these tales were previously included in my two-volume set entitled *Pleasant Journeys: Tales to Tell from Around the World* (Mercer Island, WA: The Writing Works, 1979), and later renamed *Twenty-Two Splendid Tales to Tell From Around the World,* (Little Rock: August House, 1990).

Motifs given are from *The Storyteller's Sourcebook: A Subject, Title and Motif Index to Folklore Collections for Children* by Margaret Read MacDonald (Detroit: Neal-Schuman/Gale, 1982).

The Turnip — Russia

Motif Z49.9. This classic, energetic, Russian tale is guaranteed to engage the very young. It's a fine choice to begin a story program because it models the importance of everyone's help. Have the listeners join in on the "pulling."

See *The Great Big Enormous Turnip* by Alexei Tolstoy (New York: Watts, 1968). Also, *The Fairy Tale Treasury* by Virginia Haviland (New York: Coward, McCann & Geoghegan, 1972), pp. 44–47.

The Silly Farmer—Ethiopia

Motif J2241.1.1. Children love the silliness of this plot and react with delight to its conclusion. Change voice and gestures to portray the farmer and the witch.

Another version is found in *The Fire on the Mountain and Other Ethiopian Stories* by Harold Courlander and Wolf Leslau (New York: Holt, 1950), pp. 113–18.

For a Norwegian variation, see *Noodlehead Stories From Around the World* by Moritz A. Jagendorf (New York: Vanguard, 1957), pp. 180–83.

Close the Door!—United States

Motif J2511.0.1. This tale has been embraced by many different cultures. I first heard it the form of a popular fifteenth century English ballad called "Bar the Door!" It's derived from a story told in Persia and India.

See *Persian Folk and Fairy Tales* by Anne Sinclair Mehdevi (New York: Knopf, 1965), pp. 93–103. Also, *Noodlehead Stories From Around the World* by Moritz A. Jagendorf (New York: Vanguard, 1957), pp. 34–36.

The Squire's Bride—Norway

Motif J1615. A truly funny tale that begs for

expressive gestures during the telling. When the squire first sees the bride, open your eyes as wide as your mouth.

Other versions: *Norwegian Folk Tales* by Peter Christian and Jørgen Moe Asbørnsen (New York: Viking, 1960), pp. 56–60. *True and Untrue and other Norse Tales* by Sigrid Undset (New York: Knopf, 1945), pp. 209–12.

The Extraordinary Cat—China

Motif L392.0.4. I often introduce this tale by asking listeners the names of their cats. In the telling I emphasize the line, "The children were the wisest of all..." It's the children who invariably end the story for me by shouting, "CAT!"

See: *The Toad is the Emperor's Uncle: Animal Folktales from Viet-Nam* by Vo-Dinh (Garden City, NY: Doubleday, 1970), pp. 123–28. *The King Who Rides a Tiger and Other Folk Tales from Nepal* by Patricia Hitchcock (Berkeley, CA: Parnasus, 1966), pp. 53–60.

The Man Who Was on Fire Behind—Switzerland

K300. Courting stories of old seldom reflect today's customs as well as this one. Independent and contemporary, Greta is a strong role model. I heard this tale in the living room of a Swiss grandmother in Seattle, in 1972. And though it has all the markings of a traditional folktale, I haven't been successful in tracing its print origin.

Two Wives—India

Motif J2112.2. This tale was told by Aesop. Before sharing, I explain how marriage customs have culturally differed throughout history. During the telling, I amplify the wives' power by playing their roles to the hilt. It always produces welcome laughter!

Other versions: *Noodlehead Stories From Around the World* by Moritz A. Jagendorf (New York: Vanguard, 1957), pp. 24–29. *Aesop's Fables* by Aesop (New York: Viking, 1933), pp. 78–79.

The Bear Who Said North—Finland

Motif K561.1.0.5. A great story for facial expressions! Clench your teeth and draw out the final word: "EEEeeeeaaaasssssstttt!"

See: *Tales From a Finnish Tuppa* by James Cloyd Bowman and Margery Bianco (Chicago: Albert Whitman, 1936, 1965), p. 257. *The Shepherd's Nosegay: Stories from Finland and Czechoslovakia* by Parker Fillmore (New York: Harcourt, Brace & World, 1919, 1958), pp. 69–71.

The Proud Fox — United States

Motif J2351.1. In my introduction to this tale, I ask young listeners to define the word "pride." The responses are wide and varied. One second-grade boy said it was the name of his breakfast cereal. After the story, I ask again. The fresh responses are always impressive.

A European version is found in *European Folk and Fairy Tales* by Joseph Jacobs (New York: Putnam, 1916, 1967), pp. 42–50.

For a Russian version, see *Tales From Atop a Russian Stove* by Janet Higonnet-Schnopper (Chicago: Albert Whitman, 1973), pp. 76–81.

Three Wishes — Sweden

Motif J2075.1. I ask both young and older listeners what they would want if given the gift of three wishes. The responses vary from a new mountain bike to world peace. It's when a generous person replies "better health for my sister," or "a vacation for my mother," that I'm ready to begin this story. Have fun enacting the "sausage-pull."

For other retellings, see *Once Upon a Time: Twenty Cheerful Tales to Read and Tell* by Rose Dobbs (New York: Random, 1950), pp. 86–90; and *More Celtic Tales* by Joseph Jacobs (New York: Putnam, 1902), pp. 107–9.